Text & Images
© Mia Melesina Granger

Edited by Highschool Horror

January 2023

Typesetting ©
Highschool Horror
highschoolhorror.com
Highschool Horror is an imprint of
Veneficia Publications

THE RED BOX

MIA MELESINA GRANGER

As long as I was happy, and had my friends: Amarta, Venus, and Mirya, nothing else mattered to me.

Venus and Mirya had hazel, brown eyes, and were around the same height. Venus was a dark brunette, while Mirya was a silly blonde.

Amarta had jet, black, hair with big blue eyes and freckles across her nose. She was smaller than the other two girls. She was also the prettiest, and my closest friend.

Amarta, Mirya, and Venus were coming round to mine for a sleepover. It was my birthday, so it made sense that they would stay the night.

That morning, I remember more than anything else, because I should've cherished it.

One foot at a time, I stepped out of my bed and went straight for a shower, I couldn't stop thinking about how much fun I was going to have. I showered as fast as I could, remembering to wash properly of course, and walked back inside my small bedroom, to get dressed. I chose a pair of brown, baggy, jeans and a dark green, tight, vest top. I added some rings, and necklaces and took one last look at myself.

"You're 15" I whispered to myself in the mirror. "I can't believe you're 15."

As soon as I ran down the stairs and slid my way into the kitchen, my dad was there, ready with snacks, and drinks and so many different films to watch.

I absolutely loved my dad, to the moon and back, he was my superhero, but even superheroes have a dark side, right? His was drinking too much, making him short tempered. Well, maybe not heroes like batman or Spiderman, but my dad did.

I don't blame him, mum's gone, so of course it's going to be hard for him to raise me by himself. I'd irritate him by talking too loud on the phone with Amarta, or when he couldn't hear me when I said something to him.

Also, he'd shout at me for leaving my clothes on the floor and not cleaning my room. Loudly. But Id understand why, I was annoying him. But why then, did I feel like *he* didn't love me?

"Good morning my cherry cheeks!" Said my dad in a happy tone.

"'Morning Dad, what time are the girls getting here?" I asked him.

"Don't be so impatient all the time, you can wait for them like I waited for you to get out of bed" he continued, the happy tone, quickly leaving his voice. I never understood why dad didn't like me. I understood why I irritated him, but more than anything I just wanted him to like me.

As I went to answer, the door knocked, and I went to open it. I already knew who would be standing there. The door creaked open, and Amarta and Mirya were on the doorstep with their bags in their hands. I hugged them before welcoming them inside.

"Where's Venus?" I asked.

"She, said she was going to be a bit late because, her mum had to pick up their dog from the vets" Myra answered. I understood, and texted Venus to text me back when she was on her way, she replied with the usual, "will do xx".

It wasn't like Venus to be late, if anything, she'd be early, but I shrugged it off and waited for Dad to talk to their parents.

When Mirya, and Amarta's parents left, we all went into the kitchen, picked up our snacks, and drinks, then went up into my room. We played a few different games before Venus joined us, such as, *Never Have I Ever, Truth or Dare,* and even *Put a Finger Down.*
But then Amarta said something that caught mine and Mirya's complete, and utter attention.

"Have you heard of the chapel?" She asked.

Me and Mirya, both looked at each other, waiting for her to elaborate.

Then she continued.

"The chapel in the woods. It's apparently haunted and guarded by a ghost in a tiny, little, red box."

We heard steps coming upstairs, However, they didn't sound like my dad's, I had no idea of who it could've been. The door slowly moved towards us opening ...

"BARRRRRRHHHH!"

Someone jumped from behind the door and scared us, it was Venus. We all sat there, scared out of our wits.

"Venus! We thought you were a ghost!" shouted Amarta.

"Why would you think I was a ghost you Dum Dum?" I explained.

"Because Amarta was telling us about this haunted chapel in the middle of the woods. Apparently there's a ghost, or even spirit who lives in a little red box."

The room fell silent, Venus sat on the bed watching the looks on our faces as Amarta explained.

"Let's go there." I said

And so, it was decided that we were all going to go into the woods to find the red box. We knew it could be fake, but it could be real, and in that case, it would make sense to go and find it. If we did, we could be in the paper, or famous or something ...

"What time are we going?" I asked. The other 2 girls stared at Amarta, waiting for an answer.

"Tonight, at 11:00pm, by then your dad will be asleep and we can sneak out of the window."

Her plan was well thought out, we all agreed on that. So, we went along with it and waited until 11:00pm.

"Girls, could you come down here please?!"
Shouted my dad. We all traipsed down the
stairs to the front room.

"What would you guys like for dinner?" he
asked. We all looked at each other knowing
exactly what we wanted.

"Kimparium please" we laughed. Kimparium
was a delicious restaurant that did take
out. It was a Pasta place, which had
several different types of pasta and a
range sides to go with it. It was our
favourite.

"Wonderful choice, I'll order it now." he
said agreeing with us. We were all so
excited, we couldn't remember the last
time we had Kimparium, it might've been
at Mirya's birthday party, where we went
to the restaurant itself.
"Dawn, could you stay down here a minute
please?" I wasn't a big fan of my name,
it meant light. Most people say my name
is lovely, but I don't like it.

Amarta, Venus, and Mirya went upstairs
while my dad talked to me.

"I don't think you should eat dinner
tonight" he said. "You're getting a little
bit too big, no one wants to be seen with
a fat friend or daughter, do they?" I
could understand what he meant by that,
but it hurt me.

"But dad, I haven't had Kimparium in ages, can't I just eat it this one time?" I asked him.

His face grew angry and red, and I knew what he was going to do. He lifted his hand in the air and lowered down towards me. I covered my face in defence ...

Amarta saw it all from the top of the stairs.

"Oh my god Dawn, Mirya just made up the greatest game ever, you have to come and play." Amarta said to me with a worried look on her face. As I went upstairs, my dad looked even more angry at Amarta saving me. She knew exactly what my dad was going to do. As soon as we got upstairs, I started to cry. Amarta had known that my dad was going to hit me.

"Dawn, you never told us your dad hits you?" said Amarta worried. The two other girls stared at me in complete shock. They looked concerned and walked over to hug me as I cried.

"It's a good thing we're sneaking out tonight, Dawn can get away from her dad and we can all have some girl time trying to find a dangerous spirit" giggled Mirya. We all laughed at what Mirya said and agreed that sneaking out would probably be the best thing to do. Little did we know; it was the worst choice we had ever made in our lives!

We had dinner, played more games, watched a few films, and got into our beds and waited for the chance to sneak out.

"You girls go straight to sleep okay?" said dad before closing the door on us.

"Goodnight." we all replied.

We stayed up and chatted for about an hour before getting dressed into our warmer clothes and heading out.

"Be careful climbing out," Amarta said.

We used our sleeping bags to make a rope to climb out of the window. Looking back on it now, it wasn't extremely safe. I was the last one out of the window, jumping onto the grass beneath and landing on my tiptoes. And so, we all started following Amarta as she knew where to go.

"Amarta?" I questioned.

"What forest are we going to?"

"Deadman Forest. Why?" she replied.

Deadman Forest had been closed off for 5 years after a murdered body was discovered there. The original name of the place was 'Bed knock Forest' however after the murdered body was uncovered, people began referring to it as Deadman Forest.

"No Amarta! Why are we going there we'll get caught?" asked a worried Venus.

"No, we won't. We'll be fine. Besides, it's only a 30-minute walk from here." Amarta said calmly. We all stared at her annoyed.

"30 MINUTES!"
We were walking for ages, and it definitely felt much longer than 30 minutes. But then I guess, to four teenagers, who were probably walking in the wrong direction, it would seem ages.

"How much longer?" Mirya asked, out of breath.

"Not much longer I think," replied Amarta. Venus, Mirya, and I looked at each other knowing we were lost and turned to Amarta.

"Amarta, are we lost?"

"What? No, of course we're not lost, why would you even think that? I'm extremely capable of taking us to Deadman Forest." Amarta said in an annoyed tone. Even though we didn't know where we were, we followed Amarta without hesitation. She was the oldest in the group and we all trusted her.

"Dawn?" said Venus.

"Yeah?"

We looked at each other, but her face looked desperate. I was annoyed. Did she really need to pee?
"Venus ... you're joking?" I said hopefully.

"No, I really need to go ..."

"Venus, you should've gone before we left!" shouted Mirya. We all shushed her for making too much noise and turned back to Venus.

"Go behind the tree over there" whispered Amarta, pointing to the tree. Venus walked behind the tree, and then we heard her scream. We turned to see Venus running back, before flinging her arms around all of us.

"Th - There's someone there ..." she said terrified.

All of our eyes widened with fear, as we heard rustling from the bushes in front of us. We all stepped back, not running away, as our curiosity had definitely got the better of us. Instead, we waited for whoever was going to come out.

"H - help me please." a low voice stuttered from the bushes.

One leg, and then another stepped out, to reveal a dirty teenage boy. He looked to be the same age as us, maybe a year older, but he was filthy.

"I need help, please, I've lost my dad in the forest, and I need him back" said the boy out of breath. We looked at him as he was desperately waiting for us to say something.

"Are you girls in trouble?" He asked. He sounded sincere. So, we all nodded, and agreed to help him by taking him along.

Who knows what might happen?

He was quiet, but we could sense that he felt safe with us, which was good enough for now.

"What's your name?" I asked. The boy remained silent for a few seconds before answering.

"Chand. My name is Chand," he eventually replied.

"What does it mean?" I asked, but he didn't answer.

"Mine means immortality." Offered Amarta, "which is a bit strange, because I'm not."

We all burst out giggling before quieting down and looking at Chand.

"So, you don't know where your dad is?"

"He's missing, that's all I know." We gasped and wondered, why he was looking for his dad in Deadman's Forest?

"He's been missing for over 5 years ..." but before he could continue his sentence, Venus interrupted everyone.

"... Guys, we're here be quiet." She said quietly. All five of us stepped cautiously over the red and white tape. And moving the branches from the trees, we started walking along a muddy path.

Chand was a tall boy, with grey eyes and dark brown hair. He had freckles and a scar on his chin, and marks on his wrists but not self-harm ones. They were more like the ones I had on my wrists caused by my dad.

"You have marks too?" I asked him.

"They're from my mum—she wasn't as nice as you'd think a mum would be, but I miss her." His face, frowned as he spoke.

"Same with my dad as well, he's an alcoholic, so he gets angry a lot"

Chand and I were very alike. His mum had died when he was 10 years old, and his dad went missing over five years ago. He was lonely. I could tell, but I, at least felt not quite as lonely as I had before.

"Is this it?" asked Mirya to Amarta.

"Yes, we're here, this is it." We all moaned about how long the walk was.

"Blimey Amarta, that took ages, you said 30 minutes!" Venus shouted.

"Don't shout, let's look for the box" I responded with a sigh.

We all searched for the red box, but not finding anything. We looked through the trees, in the bushes, under rocks, everywhere. At least that's what we thought.

"Could it be under the ground?" commented Chand.

A good idea finally appeared out of nowhere. I mean, us group of girls wouldn't have gotten very far with a task like that. After Chand spoke, he picked up a rusty shovel that was sticking out of the ground next to him and smiled at us. We all picked up rocks and thick sticks to help with digging the dry, compacted, dirt.

It had been 10 minutes and as far as we were concerned it was taking up too much time. I Went over to see Chand as I wanted to ask him something.

"Chand, do you know what people call this forest?" I asked him, but before he could answer, there was a thud ...

Chand looked towards us, where the thud had come from. We looked at each other.

He plunged the shovel into the ground once more, and the same thudding sound was heard. He started digging around a solid lump in the ground and I noticed a bit of red. I called the girls over while Chand continued digging.

"We've found it! Come on. We've found it!" I shouted in excitement. That moment seemed absolutely incredible.

We all helped Chand with the box, however, it was way bigger than we expected, definitely not a little box.

"Why is it so big?" asked Venus.
"And so heavy?" continued Mirya.

We all carried the box and placed it on
top of a big rock before opening it. All
of us were interested in what could be
inside it, and our hands were all itching
to open the box. It had fancy designs on
it, with swirls and leaves of gold
embedded in it.

"Do you want to do the honours Dawn, as
it's your birthday?" Amarta said to me.

As I moved my hands towards the box, I
could feel the air thicken in-between my
fingers, however, I was still able to open
it. I unclipped it and slowly lifted the
lid. the soft material inside was ruby red
coloured. It looked brand new. A volcano

of dark smoke came shooting out the box, up towards the sky and danced around us creating a cage of mysterious darkness. Suddenly these tall, thin, figures lined up around us, trapping us in the centre.

I held onto Chand and Amarta while Mirya and Venus were crying behind us. We all faced the box. These figures were over 7ft tall, with their mouths open: screeching, and wide eyed.

"CLOSE THE BOX!" I shouted.

The figures became louder and louder, screeching, and our ears felt like they would burst. Amarta ran over to the box to shut it, but something caught her arm, twisting it until the bone cracked. We all witnessed her screams of pain but didn't dare to go near her. All we could do was shout her name.

Amarta's bone was coming out of her arm, the bone was snapped in half, and she was bleeding from her elbow. I still regret not doing anything.

"STOP, PLEASE!" she screamed out.

Finally, Chand pulled Amarta back towards us, the other two girls were still crying.

The box was now shut...

The figures were gone, the sounds had stopped, and the box was shut, but we were terrified. Amarta had a broken arm, we had nowhere to go and no one to help her. We couldn't go back to my house: God knows what my dad would've done. We couldn't go anywhere. Amarta was screaming on the floor in pain, with only us to comfort her.

Venus and Mirya were still panicking, and Chand went over to help them while I stayed with Amarta.

"Amarta, look at me, it's all going to be okay, I promise you. You're going to be okay" I reassured her.

I ripped off the bottom part of the top I was wearing and looked around for a relatively straight stick.

"This is going to really hurt but it will all be worth it." I said, but before she could answer, I straightened her arm. It made a cracking sound. Then, I took the stick, placed it on her arm and began to wrap the cloth around it. Amarta begged me to stop, and the sound of my friend begging was torture to my ears. Chand was done helping the girls, as they were much calmer now.

"We need to get out of here now and go somewhere different" said Mirya.

We all readily agreed and started to head out the forest, I stayed very close to Amarta, making sure I was with her the whole time. We crossed the red and white tape again, moving the branches of the trees that were in our way. Venus helped Amarta over while I stretched the tape down far enough for her to step over.

We were young, so very young, and not fully aware of where we were. We were terrified, hurt, tired, and we were also in danger. However, we didn't know that at the time.

"We need to go to a gas station, get more food and water, and then go to the hospital" said Venus.

"Good plan. We need to go this way," Chand pointed down a street. We had a plan, and we were going to be okay.

Walking to the gas station took ages, even longer than getting to the forest. It was as if we were going in circles the whole time.

"Isn't that the same tree we passed earlier?" asked Chand.

"No way, it must just look the same" I answered.

Something was off, very off. We were being watched, I could feel it, eyes following, our every move. I didn't say anything about it to the others, I didn't want to scare them any more than they were already. And I was sure I was probably just being paranoid.

"I'm so tired, can we take a break?" asked Amarta. We thought that was a good idea and slowly sat Amarta down on the curb.

"If we don't get food in the next 20 minutes, I'm going to eat one of you guys" said Mirya. "Surely there's some mushrooms or berries around here at least."

Berries and mushrooms didn't seem like a bad idea, we were all hungry and didn't have any other food. So, we decided to look around in the trees next to us.

"Guys look,! A bunny!" said Venus. Chand, Venus, Mirya, and Amarta stared at the rabbit as I continued looking for food. I came across a blackberry bush, a strawberry plant, and a mushroom. There was only one mushroom so I ate it before the others could see it. As I looked

deeper into the trees, I could see another type of berry bush.
Suddenly I felt something hit me and I fell to the ground, my face landing in the dirt.

"What the?" I said looking up. A black figure stared straight at me, with the widest smile imaginable.

"Well, looks like I caught you at a reasonable time." The voice was deep and sounded posh but dark. I was in shock, but moving away from this thing wasn't an option, I was completely frozen with fear.

"You are in danger, just ahead of you, you're going to drop dead and your friends also. That box is close, and it wants a new spirit. The choices you've made may have benefitted you greatly, assuming you're the one left standing."
Its words went through my head like butter. I had to do whatever it took to survive.

"I'll skin them alive if I have to. This game is one that Amarta wanted to play. I wanted no part." I replied

"Very good, I'll lead you back to where it all began." Then it grabbed me and shook me until I woke up.

"Dawn are you ok?" asked Amarta.

I sat upright.

"Oh, I'm fine, don't worry ... I just fell" I said hesitantly.

"Are you sure?" said Chand.

"Everything will be fine, I know that" I answered.

We continued to walk, eating the berries along the way. I found it odd that they were walking straight into trouble, and only I knew.

I was angry, I didn't want to find that stupid box in the first place, despite everything I would've probably had more fun with my dad, I wish I'd never had a sleepover with them.

"It was a good thing we found these berries, otherwise I think we would've eaten grass" said Amarta laughing.
"Oh, Shut up Amarta you brat." I said loudly. They all turned to look at me in surprise. They looked scared.

"Dawn ... are you feeling ok?" asked Chand.

"Yeah, I'm great" I answered sarcastically "I personally think you are all just acting stupid." Chand pulled me closer for a private talk.

"What's going on with you?" he asked.

"Don't act like you know me more than you actually do Chand, everyone is being pathetic and frankly it's boring." I said.

"What the hell are you on about?" he said raising his voice. "We're completely lost, Amarta has a broken arm, we found a weird, spooky demon box, we need to get some water, and on top of all that you're acting like the brat, not Amarta!" He shouted.

"What are you shouting at me for? You're the one who obviously has a problem, not everyone else" I said. I looked him dead in the eyes, my blood was boiling. Was he serious? He had the nerve to raise his voice at me and act like he's been here from the start. He sounded obsessed with Amarta. If the situation was as urgent as he made it sound, he wouldn't be all over Amarta.

"Sounds like all of that stuff is the least of your worries apart from Amarta!" I shouted viciously.

"W - what are you on about?" he stuttered.

"You love her don't you." I said.

There was silence. He looked shocked. He muttered something under his breath and walked off towards the other girls. I was so angry. He loved Amarta when I was there for him more. He made me sick, lovesick. However, he just wasn't worth it.

I'd started walking over to them when I immediately got hit on the head.

"Ow! What the ...?" I looked up again to see it grinning in my face.

"Surprised to see me?" It said, tilting its head to one side quickly. Its body moved like a snake, however, his head didn't.

"Poor Dawn ... left side of her heartbroken, and the right suddenly hungry for revenge. You know that he'll keep going back to her either way ... but not if she's gone forever ..." it said.

"You mean like, kill her?" I asked.

"It's the only way to prove you love him isn't it? If you can't have him, she shouldn't either ..."

"How much longer are we going to be walking for?" asked Mirya.

"Until I say so. God, you guys are so impatient." I snapped. I could sense we were close to somewhere. However, I had no idea where.

"Hey, do you guys feel a bit sick?" Chand asked"

"Very" answered Amarta.

"I think I'm going to throw up." Just as Venus said that she began vomiting all over the road, followed by Chand, Amarta, and Mirya. I, on the other hand felt fine. "Why aren't you throwing up?" They all asked.

"Well, because I don't feel sick right now?" I responded, with them still vomiting.

"Do you guys see that light over there?" I asked. It was very bright, like an entrance to somewhere.

"I do. Over there!" shouted Mirya.
We all sprinted towards the light, which was rapidly growing the closer we got to it. We all asked each other what we thought it was, the excitement was visible on our faces. We all felt it was something good.

Stuck going around in circles the whole time didn't help, but maybe a strange light coming from the middle of the road did. As we reached the light, it was warm, and homely. It didn't feel dangerous or bad. It felt safe. My curiosity got the very best of me as I started to step inside the light, one foot after another.

"Dawn what are you doing? Don't go!" But before Amarta could finish her sentence, I was walking into the light.

All four of them came through the light after me.

"W - what are we doing back here?" Venus asked.

"Why are we here? Why are we back?" Shouted Mirya, her eyes starting to prick with tears, I could tell they were scared.

"So, this is what it was talking about" I thought. "It brought us back here."

"Dawn what the hell are you talking about?" Shouted Amarta. I turned to the big rock, to see the box once again. I couldn't help it; it was like I was being controlled. I inched towards it, step by step, my hands itching to open the lid once again.

Something made me open that box.

I walked over to it, everyone screaming at me to step away from it, but my hands were on the lid, and I threw it open.

Nothing happened.

"Why was nothing happing?"

"Because everything is now up to you," a familiar voice said, as it suddenly, appeared from behind me.

"Pleased to see me I can tell. However, don't get too excited yet, you know why I'm here. It's time to sacrifice them. You've done so well getting them all here, and now you can do the honours, and push them into the box" it smiled.

"I can't thank you enough for bringing my boy along on your journey, I can tell he's been having fun with you all."

My eyes couldn't have been any wider.

"D - do you mean Chand?" I asked.

"Of course, he's my son, and I'm so grateful that you helped him out, he wouldn't stop looking for me in these bloody woods." I was completely shocked. That thing was Chand's dad. The spirit that followed me since we were last in the forest. That was Chand's dad!

"Who exactly are you again?" I asked it, wanting to know more.

"Oh, my. My manners have completely disappeared. I'm the spirit in that box" it grinned.
My thoughts were all over the place.

How was I going to tell Chand?" No, I couldn't. Besides, he doesn't even care about me, he cares more about Amarta.

"So, if I push them into the box, what will happen to you?" I asked him.

I'll have my freedom back, and be a free spirit, and they'll take my place. The more people in the box, the more freedom I get" it replied.

"So, what's in it for me?"

"I'll do something in return for you —a wish of your choice." It kept on smiling at me.

Nothing was stopping me. I could get rid of them and get something in return, easy.

"Okay, deal."

"DAWN!" shouted Mirya. "Why did you open the box again?"

"Look, nothing's happening, see? Come look." I told them.

They came further forward as I reached my hand towards them for support. Venus inched over toward the box to see inside. In an instant, her head was blown up, like a bomb exploding. Everyone screamed as Venus's blood went all over us.
"VENUS!" shouted Mirya. She dropped to the floor and started crying, while Venus' headless body fell to the ground like a rock.

Sounds of weeping filled the forest as the sleeping birds fled their nests. Of course, Mirya was crying, Venus was her best friend, but that didn't matter to me at the time.

"Right, who's next?" I asked smiling.

"Dawn what the hell is wrong with you? You psycho?!" Shouted Amarta.

"Oh, wouldn't you love to know, it's a shame you'll never find out since your head is always up Chand's ass!" I shouted. I was so angry at her. She *really* thought she was innocent.

"Dawn you know that's not the truth." Said Chand.

Mirya was still crying.

"Oh, shut up Mirya! If you're so sad about Venus why don't you go join her?" I said.

I grabbed her wrist and tugged on her to get her nearer to the box, she screamed and shouted at me to stop, but it didn't work. I was always stronger than Mirya, even when we were younger. We would play tug of war and I would always win.

"Please Dawn, don't do this. I'm begging you I can't die!" She sobbed but it was too late.

She was an inch away from the box when her neck broke, forcing it to the left, and resting it on her shoulder. Little cracks were heard from her body, the sound of all her bones breaking. She fell to the floor, rolling around in pain, her screaming filling the forest. She started to calm down and her screams went quiet. No more movement. She was gone. Two down, and two to go.

Amarta was next, she deserved it after everything she had done. I started slowly walking towards her, and she backed away with every step I took. I could tell she was scared, but I didn't care, the sooner I got rid of her the better.
Chand suddenly stepped in front of me.

"Dawn what the hell is going on with you? Why are you killing your friends?" He seemed sincere but at the same time angry.

"Oh, come on, don't act like you care now!
You've been obsessing over Amarta from the
moment we found you in that bush. You have
no idea how much that hurt. Yes I barely
know you, but I feel like I've known you
my entire, life. I've never met anyone as
amazing, smart, caring, funny, and brave
as you Chand. I love you."

I could feel the blood rushing through my
body, my palms were starting to sweat, and
my ears were getting hot. I could feel my
heart beating like a drum. How could I
have been so stupid as to tell him that?
Chand stared at me, he looked sorry for
me. I was terrified what he was going to
say. Did I say the wrong thing?

"Dawn" he said. "You know when we were
walking along the road, after we found the
berries. You were being rude to everyone,
so I talked to you in private? You accused
me of being in love with Amarta. After
that, I mumbled and walked away."
"Yeah I remember that" I said quietly. I
was too scared to raise my voice after
what I had just said to him.

"I love you, not Amarta ... that's what I
mumbled when I walked away."

I stuttered before I could give a proper
reply.

"B - But I thought, you loved Amarta?" I
questioned.

Amarta stood there, silently before
slapping me around the face.

"You little bitch! You think I talked
behind your back about a guy, I clearly
liked too, and that's why you treated me
like you did?" She was furious.

She started pushing me towards the box,
pulling on my hair and dragging me. I
hesitated and dropped to the floor to make
her struggle. Of course, she fell as well,
and we carried on scrapping on the muddy
ground until Chand finally pulled us
apart, grabbed me round my waist, pushing
Amarta away from us both.

"STOP FIGHTING!" He bellowed.

"Amarta, I think you're amazing, you're
nice and caring, but you're not for me,
and I'm sorry about that. Dawn, I know
I've hurt you, and I hate myself for that.
I want to show you how much you really
mean to me." He said.

His arms left my waist as they travelled
towards Amarta. What was he doing? He
grabbed Amarta by her waist and leaned in
to kiss her, but just before he could, he
shoved Amarta away, pushing her body
toward the box. Suddenly lightning struck

hitting a tree; the flames caught hold of the leaves and the smoke rose high into the air. The tree started moving, falling to the left, and getting closer and closer to Amarta. She screeched in horror as she was crushed by the tree, the flames from it reaching for her flesh. She started to burn with the tree on top of her. However, we could still see her face as it burned, turning red, as it rapidly cooked.

Chand and I stared at each other until we heard sirens in the distance, growing louder and louder. We heard the police and their dogs, but we didn't move. We just stayed there, looking at the bodies of my once 'best friends.'

MONDAY 13TH OF DECEMBER 2039

"That's how it all happened. I know it's taken a long time to get it out of me, but that's exactly what happened, just as I remember it."

"Dawn you've been in therapy for about 18 years. Why has it taken you this long to tell us what really happened that day?"

"Because I felt like you wouldn't believe me, or my boyfriend. You would've thought we were lying to you, but you weren't there that day. We were just a couple of young silly teenagers who didn't know what to do. But I don't regret what I did. I did it for a reason. I did it because he told me to."

"Who Dawn? Who told you to?"
"The man with the smile. The man with the big eyes. The man that told me I'd get whatever I wanted. He lied. I'm in a mental institution. That's not what I wanted, talking to you every day until I'm cured is NOT what I wanted."

"Now Dawn calm down. I'm sorry about what happened, we'll send a search team out to look for that box and if we find it, we'll get rid of it, does that sound good?"

"You can't get rid of it. It's not a toy, it's a curse. Whatever spirit is in that box now, will get inside your mind and turn it around. It will change your whole personality. The way you talk, the way you walk, the way you eat, sleep, drink, and think. It will change you. Trust me, I still don't know who I was before that spirit got inside my brain. And that's why I'm here now. Whoever is in that box will manipulate you until it's satisfied. It always knows where you are, and it won't leave you with your thoughts. Please believe me when I say this ...

...It always finds you."

HIGHSCHOOL HORROR

**TEENAGE HORROR/THRILLER STORIES
WRITTEN & ILLUSTRATED BY
TEENAGERS FOR TEENAGERS**

PLEASE SUBMIT YOUR STORIES TO:

highschoolhorror.com

highschoolhorror@gmail.com

Highschool Horror is an imprint of Veneficia Publications

The Power of the Young Author

HIGHSCHOOL HORROR WORKSHOP

FOR
TEENS AND YOUNG ADULTS INTERESTED IN WRITING HORROR/THRILLER FICTION

THIS IS A **FREE** WORKSHOP AIMED AT ALL THOSE DARK YOUNG SOULS INTERESTED IN SHARING THEIR MACABRE STORIES WITH OTHER DARK SOULS !!!

WE WELCOME:
WITCHES, VAMPIRES, ZOMBIES, WEREWOLVES, GHOSTS, DEMONS AND ANYTHING ELSE THAT GOES BUMP IN THE NIGHT.

HIGHSCHOOL HORROR WORKSHOPS ARE FUN EVENTS AIMED AT PROVIDING YOUNG ADULTS AIMED 11 YEARS UPWARDS CULTIVATE THEIR IDEAS INTO STORIES AND GRAPHIC NOVELS (COMIC BOOK FORMAT). AS WELL AS GAIN THE EXPERIENCE OF WORKING WITH AN ESTABLISHED PUBLISHING HOUSE. IF YOU ARE INTERESTED IN HOLDING AN EVENT IN YOUR AREA AND KNOW OF A VENUE, OR ARE A SCHOOL OR CLUB, THEN PLEASE GET IN TOUCH.

WORKSHOPS ARE BETWEEN 1 AND 2 HOURS, DEPENDING ON NUMBERS ATTENDING.

MINIMUM ATTENDANCE IS 7 YOUNG ADULTS.

AREAS CURRENTLY COVERED ARE DORSET, HAMPSHIRE, ISLE OF WIGHT, DEVON, AND CORNWALL.

highschoolhorror.com

highschoolhorror@gmail.com

www.ingramcontent.com/pod-product-compliance
Lightning Source LLC
Chambersburg PA
CBHW052014190726
48295CB00013BA/643